Her Own Patch
of Rain

To Sue
a. Helen Baylon
12/13/15

Her Own Patch
of Rain

The Prayer of a Young Daughter

A. Helen Baylor

Pleasant Word
A Division of WinePress Group
PW

Pleasant Word (a division of WinePress Publishing, PO Box 428, Enumclaw, WA 98022) functions only as book publisher. As such, the ultimate design, content, editorial accuracy, and views expressed or implied in this work are those of the author.

Unless otherwise indicated, all Scriptures are taken from the *New King James Version*. Copyright ©1979, 1980, 1982 by Thomas Nelson, Inc. Used by permission. All rights reserved.

The folk art quilt cover design is by the author.

ISBN 13: 978-1-4141-1370-8
ISBN 10: 1-4141-1370-6
Library of Congress Catalog Card Number: 2008911185

This book is dedicated to the memory of my brother George W. Chandler, my sister Katie Richardson, and my spiritual sister and encourager Lynne Henrich.

Contents

Acknowledgments   ix

Chapter One: The Promise   1
Chapter Two: The Ritual   5
Chapter Three: The Lost Son   9
Chapter Four: The Seeds in Mother's Room   17
Chapter Five: The Lost Sunday   21
Chapter Six: The Dress   23
Chapter Seven: The Last Watering   29
Chapter Eight: A Prayer for the Rain Dance   35
Chapter Nine: The Living Water   39
Chapter Ten: Mother's Story   49
Chapter Eleven: Watering With Mother   57
Chapter Twelve: The Winter   59
Chapter Thirteen: The Ritual   63
Chapter Fourteen: Father's Story   67
Chapter Fifteen: The Confession   73

Scripture References for Further Reading   77

Acknowledgments

I THANK GOD for those who have contributed to the completion of this book. This includes those who have encouraged me over the years to keep telling my stories. These include my Sister, Elaine Harris whose literary works have also been a source of inspiration to me; Antionette Thompson who presented to me as a gift one of the journals in which I kept many of the insights that are included in this story; and more recently, my son, Shannon Baylor whose enthusiasm regarding my stories inspired me to move forward.

Those who have been a constant source of encouragement and support during this particular project are my sons, Reginald and Trenton Baylor who have both supported and inspired me with their artistic expertise, while Elouise Baylor's technical support evolved into a partnership as she came to love the project as her own. I also appreciate the diligent help of Evelyn Walker and Adrienne Walker.

My advance readers' critiques and encouragement have been invaluable. My first reader was Sheilia Payton whose journalistic experiences proved to be priceless. Denise Vielehr,s experiences as an author have also been a source of enrichment. Cindy Brey has been supportive in more ways than one. Others include Susan Krause, Katie Jackson, Jacquelyne Baylor, Robbyne Baylor, Linda Weber, Michelle Schneider, Lorene Meyer, Bonnie Duer, and Wendy Seaman.

Support comes in many forms, so I must not neglect to thank my husband for taking on an extra portion of responsibilities, such as keeping a steady supply of hot nourishing soups available. Anna Townes had no idea that the book she sent would have such power, nor did SW know the power that her enthusiasm for the story would have. I'm grateful for the steady supply of inspiring articles and cards from June Kelm. And I must not forget the prayers of all my Bible study sisters.

MICHAEL STORMED THROUGH the door in a fit of anger—again. Katie and I stood at the window that faced the street and watched him drive away. He drove out of the driveway, skidding from side to side, driving way too fast on the icy pavement.

Katie sighed and looked at me, her eyes asking for some assurance that everything was going to work out. She looked so much like Mother with those long, puffy braids and those deep dimples that appeared in her cheeks when she smiled—just like those in Mother's cheeks when she smiled. But I'd seen that smile less and less in recent months. This was the fourth time her father had stormed out, and each time he stayed away longer than the time before. That was too much for an eleven-year-old to have to struggle with. *She won't have to worry about any sadness on my face, I thought, for with the help of God, I'll be all right no matter how this turns out.* But I was worried about her, for I couldn't bear to see the sadness in her eyes that I had often seen in mother's eyes—especially during the summer I was Katie's age.

I hadn't told Katie about that summer. But if ever there was a time to tell her, it was at that moment. So I put my arm around her waist and guided her over to the sofa.

When the daylight lasted just the right number of hours, and the sun had warmed the soil just enough, its light bounced off the clay hill along the side of the road in front of our house, beckoning Florence, 15; Sammy, 13; and me, 11, to begin our yearly quest up the hill in search of the "sour things."

We had climbed the hill for the first time when we were small children venturing beyond the boundaries set by Mother. We had climbed it simply for the challenge—and to stand triumphantly upon its plateau and bask in the victory of small conquerors.

But we discovered a patch of long and thin green stems, most having umbels of three tear-shaped leaves at the top, with a few having four. With the curiosity and daring of children, and with Sammy's prompting, we tasted them and named them the "sour things." We made our trek each year after that.

On the day of our ritual that spring we climbed the hill, which no longer felt nearly as tall as it did the first time we climbed it, and we followed the now familiar path with certainty that the sour things would be there.

Sammy took the lead as usual, and he was the first to see the patch in the clearing surrounded by bushes and tall grasses.

"Here they are!" he exclaimed excitedly. "They came back. I knew they'd still be here!"

I gazed at the delicate leaves atop their swaying stems as they waved in the breeze.

"Let's taste," Sammy prompted. I could tell that he wanted us to share the first taste, but I could not resist stealing a little more time to bend over and sweep my palms across their tops and feel their softness.

Then we each plucked a bundle and squeezed the stems until the juice glistened on our fingertips. We folded the bundles into our mouths and stood there with the exciting taste of sour in our mouths and with the warm spring sun shining on our faces, with no hint that anything was about to change.

Chapter Two

The Ritual

THAT NIGHT I lay restlessly in bed as Florence slept on the other side. I listened to the sounds I had heard once before coming from Mother's and Father's room. Their voices were loud, and their words rushed from their mouths simultaneously, mingling together in such chaos that I could not understand anything they were saying. This time, though, I heard Father say, "I give up, Clara! I give up!" The next day was to be the day of their ritual.

I grew excited when I awoke that day to find Father in the garden, wearing his field overalls and holding his shovel poised to dig and turn the next clump of dirt. He seemed so tall to me then, towering above anything that threatened to take away my joy. I let the door slam as I moved out onto the side porch that faced the west where the garden was situated and sat on the top step to watch Father perform this ritual that had been performed each spring for as long as I could remember. Grandpa said it had been going on from the day Father and Mother arrived at this, their first home. They had spent their first year of marriage with him

5

The Lost Son

FATHER HAD RETURNED by the end of the day when Mother called us to supper. We took our usual places around the table. Father and Mother sat on opposite sides of the table, but there was a heavy silence between them that was unlike the usual laughter that Father almost always brought with him when he talked about the funny things Sammy had said or the smile on his face as he reported the first sight of newly germinated corn. Nor were there the quick smiles Mother gave in response. Sammy sat on Father's right and Florence on Mother's right. I sat on Mother's left across from Florence and next to Sammy. We sat silently at first, and I was grateful for the calm of the peach colored walls surrounding us and the pink floral curtains at the window. Eventually Father said, "Let's give thanks," in a sad weak voice I had never heard him use before.

"Thank you Father, for this food that you have prepared for the nourishment of our bodies," he spoke in the same strange tone.

Knowing that he was to say his Bible verse next, Sammy recited, "The Lord is my shepherd, I shall not want."

Then Florence spoke, "In the beginning God created the heavens and the earth."

Before my turn came, Mother spoke, "Rise Peter, kill and eat."

Not liking the attention directed toward me, I spoke my short verse, "Jesus wept."

The comforting smell of the skillet-sized flapjacks and scrambled eggs filled the room. And the clinking of forks and spoons after Mother had served all of our plates eased the awkward silence as we waited for Father to begin his usual Bible storytelling with the familiar gleam in his eyes as if he was about to reveal precious treasures that he had kept hidden for that very moment. When he finally spoke, his eyes looked deep and tired, and the strange, sad voice took charge.

"There was this rich man who had two sons," Father began. "He had set aside an inheritance for both sons. But the younger of the two asked his father to give him his share right away instead of having him wait for it. And the father gave it to him.

"Well, this son took the money, left home, wasted all of it, living a reckless life, and ended up with nothing. In fact, he had to get a job taking care of pigs and was so hungry he had to eat what he fed to the pigs.

"He eventually realized that his father's servants were better off than he was. So he prepared to go home, ask his father for forgiveness, and ask to be hired as one of the servants.

"However, when the father saw him coming, he welcomed him lovingly, giving him the garments of a son—not those of a servant—and ordered a feast to be prepared in celebration of the son's return."

By now, Father's voice was becoming more alive, and the excitement was returning to his eyes.

"Well," he continued, "the older brother was angry. He reminded his father that despite his hard work and faithfulness, there had never been a feast prepared for him. But the father explained to him that the other son was lost and now he was found, as if he were alive after being dead.

"Well, the older son wasn't thinking about how the father would indeed have done the same thing for him had he been in the same situation, for he was just that kind of father—forgiving, just as God is with us."

"Was that fair?" Sammy asked.

"Well," Father lovingly replied, "the older son thought he deserved more, but he still could not do enough to deserve what his father had put aside for him. His inheritance was the gift of a loving father, like the grace that God gives his children."

We all ate silently after that, and once we had finished, Father arose from his seat, looked across the table at Mother, and softly announced, "I'm going to take my walk."

Then, glancing quickly at Florence, Sammy, and me, he left the dining room, went out the side door to the side porch, descended the steps onto the driveway leading to the road, and headed westward.

We expected Father to take his usual path over the lanes bordering the newly planted fields while there was still light and then return home by the lane that ran north and south from the back field to the back of the barn. But when night came he had not returned. Mother sent us to search the lanes by moonlight and call out his name. But there was no response except for the scurrying of small, frightened creatures.

"Should we go and ask Uncle Willis and Aunt Peggy if they have seen him?" Florence asked Mother when we returned to the house.

"No," she answered. "You all just get ready for bed." She took another look through the side door where she had stood waiting for us. Long after Sammy, Florence, and I had gone to bed, I heard Mother lock the side door and turn out the lights.

I fell asleep picturing Father on the spring day that Grandpa told us about. I pictured him standing outside his new home with everything he loved in his presence and his joy complete except for a heavy heart for Mother. I imagined how his heart must have felt when he watched Mother holding that pack of seeds so close to her and the longing in her eyes that she thought was hidden from him. I could see the same longing. I pictured him eagerly taking up the shovel and the hoe, turning the grassy clods, loosening up the soil from the tenacious grass roots, all along picturing himself at midsummer leading Mother into her garden, his love offering in bloom, making her joy complete like his.

I remembered the joy in his smile when he stood back and admired our house for everything it held inside. And I remembered how he took walks around it when I was small, holding my hand or carrying me. We'd start from the porch on the west side of our simple rectangular-shaped house with white clapboard siding. I remember his large, warm hand steadying me as we walked down the steps, my short legs wobbling with each step.

We'd then turn north toward the front, first gazing at the zinnias just across the driveway. We'd reach the front steps to the north side of the porch that faced the road. Each step was an adventure as he helped me climb up.

"Wow, you can climb as well as I can," he'd exclaim with a chuckle. Then he'd take me to the east side where it was shady and cool in the afternoon and where I liked to touch the coolness and the roughness of the tall, red brick chimney.

"Look, there's a tomato!" he'd shout, pointing past the wire fence of the garden just a few feet from the yard. I'd rush over to take a closer look and reach through the wire and touch its smooth surface. The soft, green grass made a swishing sound as I ran to catch up with him as he started to move slowly toward the south end of the house.

By this time my legs were usually growing tired, and I looked forward to raising my arms upward and finding Father reaching down for me, lifting me up and bringing my cheek beside his. I remembered how warm his cheeks were and how far away the ground looked as I rode on his shoulders. We'd move westward along the south side of the house and then turn northward back to the side porch. As he lowered me down to the porch, he'd take another look at the zinnia garden and exclaim with wonder in his voice, "Hon, I believe those zinnias are going to be the prettiest ever this year, don't you?"

I remembered the softness with which he spoke to Mother and how he teased and wooed her with a silent language that they thought we didn't understand. I couldn't imagine Father ever wanting to leave us. So I fell asleep, confident that I would awake early the next day to find Mother and him in the garden planting the seeds.

I awoke with a start the next morning. I dressed in a hurry, my heart pounding at the possibility of finding them there. I rushed to the door only to find the garden silent and empty. I entered it feeling the sense of loss compounded as I saw the top of the soil beginning to dry out as the sun rose in the east, beginning its daily journey to the west. I regretted that the seeds had not been planted the day before while the soil was still moist so that the hard covering over them could begin to soften to release the new life inside in preparation for fulfilling their promise.

I longed for Mother and Father to appear and tell me what to do next or for Mother to simply call me inside. But it was Florence who came to the door and called me in.

"Go get Sammy," she spoke in her serious voice, "and come and eat breakfast."

We silently ate the biscuits, eggs, and preserves that Mother had taught Florence to prepare. And there was an unspoken agreement that no one would disturb Mother.

Florence, Sammy, and I spoke very little during that day and the two days that followed. But we moved about as if we were caught up in a rhythm orchestrated by the sun. With Mother and Father there to tell us what to do, I hadn't noticed that this rhythm was there. But we knew what to do and how important it was to carry on. And it was during these three days that I learned that every living thing was caught up in this rhythm, and it either participated or did not flourish. So the momentum of this rhythm, sleeping and waking, planting and gathering, preparing, eating, tending, and nurturing kept us moving in the absence of the commands of Mother and Father. I imagined how proud Mother and Father would be when they asked if the animals had been fed and the cows milked or if Florence had prepared the meals and if I had helped. I imagined how proud we would be when the answer to every question would be "Yes, ma'am" or "Yes, sir."

After three days in her room, Mother emerged on the fourth day at sunrise, calling from the hallway, "You all get up. It's time to get up."

But something was missing in her voice. Later at the table, when I searched her face, it was serious, and her eyes seemed distant. Her movements, however, were strong and determined. She questioned each one of us individually.

"Did you keep everything fed, Sammy?" she asked.

"Yes, ma'am," he replied.

"Did you all get plenty to eat?" she asked, glancing over at Florence.

"Yes, ma'am," Florence quickly answered, hurrying to add more information while she still had Mother's attention. "I cooked biscuits just like you taught me. And we had eggs and preserves, and beans and tomatoes from the pantry."

Mother nodded her approval then glanced at me. "Did you gather the eggs and help Florence in the kitchen and look after the vegetable garden?" She asked, looking my way.

"Yes, ma'am," I proudly responded.

Mother looked intently at each of us as if we had taught her something new and pleasant. Then she fixed her gaze on me and with a smile said, "Go get the seeds, Hon. We'd better get the zinnias planted."

A combination of hope and questions flooded through me. What drew Mother out of the cocoon of her room into the harsh reality of Father's absence? Was it the realization that she couldn't flourish there? Was it the rising sun calling her back into the rhythm? Was it the waiting soil with its rich, moist darkness turning grey and hard as it lay drying in the sun? Or was it Sammy, Florence, and me? Whenever I looked into her room during those three days, I found her gaze fixed on the road, not the garden and not on me.

Chapter Four

The Seeds
in Mother's Room

IKNEW EXACTLY where the seeds were as I entered
Mother and Father's room, thinking about how the room
spoke more about her than about him. We only referred to
it as "their room" when he was there with her. As I entered,
my excitement allowed me to pay little attention to the
mahogany bed on my right that was covered with a frayed
quilt with once bright pink, yellow, and blue squares that
had faded into almost the same shade of grey. I did notice
the tall mahogany wardrobe on the left with the milk glass
vase resting on the top that would hold this summer's bouquets as it had in summers past. Straight ahead was a broad
window overlooking the driveway that led to the dirt road
running in front of our house. I could see the zinnia garden
just across the driveway. Under the window was Mother's
sewing machine, positioned so that she could look out at
intervals, especially when the zinnias were blooming. To the
right of the sewing machine in a small space between the
wall and the foot of the bed was a long table that held yards
of brightly colored fabrics cut into circles, squares, triangles,

17

and all sorts of shapes that spilled from baskets and burst through cracks in cardboard boxes. In Mother's hand, this chaos and confusion would become colorful and intricately patterned quilts that resembled scattered rainbows.

I felt privileged to be in this consecrated room. I seldom entered it unless I was sent or summoned. Often, when I saw Mother's face turned toward the window and her shoulders rounded into her work, I sensed a silent command not to disturb. There was seldom anything urgent enough for Sammy to enter either, while Florence strolled in and out at will, either not sensing or ignoring the gentile barrier at the threshold. She chattered on excitedly about the 4-H baking contest or the basketball tournament the coming weekend or how Reverend Freeman's handsome son looked admiringly at her the past Sunday when she wore the new dress Mother had made for her. Florence could coax a smile and even laughter from Mother on these brief unannounced visits before Mother's hands returned to the rhythmic motion of sewing and quilting or before her foot began rocking the peddle of the sewing machine. I preferred to enter this retreat bearing gifts whenever possible.

My most constant gift was a bouquet from the garden. We both loved the zinnias, and it was through them that I came to know the little that I did know about Mother. It was with these bouquets that I had the power to still her hands, stop the pedals, silence the humming, and bring her eyes into mine and see her dimples deepen as she smiled at me.

I moved past the fireplace on my left that was in the center between the wardrobe and the closet door and eagerly entered the closet. I felt into the dark corner of the top shelf where the seeds, harvested the previous summer, were always kept. I found them in a small paper bag, rolled up and tied with a piece of jute twine, then placed inside a jar and sealed.

I hurried back to the kitchen, but Mother had already gone out the screen door to the side porch and to the side of the barn and retrieved the rake. She was standing at the edge of the garden waiting for me and the seeds.

Mother took the top of the rake handle and drew it along the top of the first row, forming a straight shallow trench, then beckoned me to start sprinkling the seeds along it, checking my work every few feet.

"Don't plant them too thick," she warned. "But make sure you're putting enough in case some of them don't sprout." There was a sort of numbness in her voice. Once she was confident that I had learned the process, she moved on from row to row, with me following behind her. I marveled at the miracle of those tiny flat seeds gliding weightlessly from my fingers. I marveled at how they could grow into plants reaching up to Father's knees and turn this whole garden into a sea of bright reds, pinks, oranges, and yellows.

Mother and I didn't really share the planting as I imagined we would. Mother's movements were perfunctory. Nor did we stand together and share our dreams of how the zinnias would look that summer, as she and Father always did. And when she left the garden, I remembered that something had been missing in her response to Father's leaving. There was no panic or desperation as one would have whose loved one had disappeared and was possibly in danger or even worse. There was no calling us together to pray like she did when Sammy cut his heel on a piece of glass out by the woodpile and Father rushed him away to the hospital with blood gushing from his heel and tears and snot mingling above his lips and running down his face.

Mother, Florence, and I stood on the porch, almost paralyzed until the idea suddenly came to her. "Come on, let's go in and pray," she urged us, shaking both of our shoulders as if to wake us from our stupor. She hurried inside, and we followed.

There was no bargaining with God like she did in that prayer, "Lord, if you'll just take care of him and keep him safe, I'll…" Instead, she wore the posture of one betrayed— one who had to face a painful truth about something or someone he or she had trusted and depended on. Something seemed to have shattered a barrier that she wore hidden inside of her that protected a part of her that was already wounded. I think she knew Father had simply decided to leave.

I don't think she noticed the next morning that a soft rain had fallen during the night while we slept, soaking the soil and softening the dry crust that protected the tiny germ inside each seed and preparing it to sprout. I don't think she noticed the warm sunshine that morning that warmed the earth and would nurture the new sprouts as they started their journey to the light.

C h a p t e r   F i v e

The Lost Sunday

SATURDAY CAME, AND Mother said nothing about our usual Saturday morning preparations for Sunday school and church the next day. But Florence and I went through the motions of making preparations anyway. We chose the already washed and stiffly starched white shirts that Father and Sammy always wore and laid out Mother's blue and yellow floral print dress to be ironed. Florence chose her white eyelet sundress, and I chose my yellow dress with the pleated skirt and the sash that tied into a big bow in the back. We sprinkled water over all the pieces then rolled them into a ball and wrapped them in an old worn out sheet and placed the bundle in the icebox so the moisture would distribute itself evenly throughout the pieces.

After supper, while the stove was still hot, we heated the heavy irons, unwrapped the bundle and took turns ironing. We chatted as we took pride in getting every inch of fabric satiny smooth. The familiar sizzle as the hot iron met the damp fabric, the steam rising from the ironing board and the smell of the heated starch, brought comforting familiarity. By the time we finished and stood back to admire the crispness and perfection of our Sunday clothes, our skin wore the familiar glaze of perspiration drawn from our skin by the heat of the kitchen combined with the heat outside. This being completed, we shared a certain burst of energy. For we had refused to give power to the menacing truth that was closing in around us-that Father might not come home and things might never be the same again.

Mother didn't rise early that Sunday morning to wake us for church. Instead, Sammy came into the kitchen just as Florence was about to start our same breakfast of eggs, biscuits, and preserves, and announced solemnly, "Mother said we aren't going to church today."

Mother appeared in the kitchen much later, after Florence had finished cooking and I had kept the dishes washed and set the table.

"Good morning," she said, glancing around the table at Florence first, then Sammy, and then me. We were already seated, but uncertain as to whether we should start eating or wait for her.

"Whenever I'm not here, you all just carry on without me," she spoke in a matter-of-fact tone, her words seeming detached from the person speaking them. She then left the room. As she left, I sensed in her tone and in her walk a resolution not to participate in the reality surrounding us after all. And I had the feeling that she was on the brink of making that decision about all of us and everything even before Father left. I had the feeling, long before that day, that there was something else that she was also refusing to face.

The Dress

FATHER HAD NOT returned that glorious morning two weeks after the planting when I awoke to find that the third rainfall had come while we slept. I awoke to the sight of lines and lines of tiny green shoots along the tops of the rows of the zinnia garden. Tiny stems stood straight up holding pairs of tear-shaped leaves opposite each other, like wings opened up to the sun.

The zinnia's journey upward to the light appeared to be less of a struggle than that of some of the plants in the vegetable garden. Unlike the zinnia, these shoots first appeared as tiny green heads on long green necks, with the heads bowed or even partially stuck in the ground. After this struggle was over, they stood straight and triumphant, having finally pushed their way through to the light, ready to challenge the sun. There was no sign of struggle for the zinnias as they appeared ready to challenge the sun much sooner.

Although Mother sat facing the garden every day, she didn't see this miracle of new life. I watched her window, hoping to catch her glance and beckon her into the garden with me, hoping that the tiny specks of green on the ground would draw her closer to marvel with me at how something so small could hold so much promise. I wanted to hear a chuckle in her voice as she grew closer and gently cautioned me, "Don't step on any of them, Hon."

"No, ma'am," I would reply, happy to have her claim and protect them with me. But whenever she looked up from her work, her glance rested on the road running east and west in front of the house.

The fourth week passed, and Father had missed seeing the cornfields he loved turn bright green and the green pastures become dappled with patches of yellow flowers.

Mother joined us at the table less and less often, and Florence handled her new role in the kitchen with a sense of dedication I had never seen in her before. She continued to make what was most familiar to her for breakfast, the biscuits that she had mastered. For the other two daily meals she cooked chicken, which she had gathered enough courage to kill, or opened jars of canned beef and pork and boiled fresh greens that she sent me to gather from the vegetable garden.

The last time Mother joined us at the table was at breakfast. She took charge, as if everything was the same, and we all acted as if Father was just out in the fields somewhere and would appear at any moment. We also pretended that we had not had many meals alone while Mother took refuge in her room.

"Say the blessing, Sammy," Mother said, nodding her head in his direction as she spoke.

Sammy didn't tell her that he had been doing this at every meal.

"Pass your plate, Hon," she said to me, giving us no time to say our verses before serving our plates and then her own.

"Your biscuits are getting even better," she said to Florence with a forced excitement in her voice that did not match the lifelessness in her eyes. Sammy talked incessantly, going from subject to subject and from joke to joke.

"Uncle Willis said we're going fishing Saturday after we finish with the chores."

"Did you hear the joke about the preacher who couldn't remember his sermon?" And before anyone could answer, "Well, there was this preacher..."

But the reality of Father's empty chair spoke loudly the truth that things weren't the same, and before long Mother excused herself from the table. I thought about how much work it is to pretend. Reality weighs heavily for a while, but in the long run it carries its own weight.

It was the evenings when Father's absence seemed most real, the time of day when the sun hung low in the west; the time of day when the shadows of our weathered barn, the trees, and Sammy's long, lanky legs cast their longest shadows on the ground before disappearing into the dark; when the sun cast its golden glow over the ground and the sides of barns and houses for a few final minutes before darkness crept in; in the evening when the echoes of children's voices rode over the relaxed evening air as the children were called inside and doors closed.

Florence appeared much older sitting there at the table with her apron on. It was hard to picture her as she had been in past summers when she taught me to jump rope, her eyes sparkling on her round face as her two long braids flew skyward with each jump then landed on her shoulders as her bare feet landed on the ground. It was hard to remember the soft, swishing sound the rope made as it whipped the soft green blades of grass on its way upward and over her head again with the carefree excitement in her voice as she chanted, *"O Mary Mack, Mack, Mack, all dressed in black, black, black."*

Florence was doing a good job of taking Mother's place, but I missed Mother. I especially missed her hands and the life they exuded. I missed their rhythmic swirl as she mixed the biscuit dough, first pouring buttermilk into a puddle in a small basin in the center of the flower mixture in the bottom of the mixing bowl, then carefully stirring in small amounts until the mixture started to bubble and rise. I missed the way her hands kneaded the dough until it was smooth and ready to be cut and baked. I missed the white cloud of flour that escaped into the air as she turned and patted the dough. I missed the sour smell of the buttermilk as it mixed with the flour. I missed the bounty that surrounded her and gave testament to the burdened but tenacious spirit within her, whether this bounty was the warm, brown bread just lifted from the oven, an intricately stitched quilt, or the zinnias that yielded the bouquets I brought her.

I missed Sundays the most. I missed Mother and Father on the front seat and Sammy, Florence, and me in the back seat of our car that Father got in a trade for his two most prized cows. I loved being with our church family. I especially missed seeing Mother with her church sisters. I liked Reverend Freeman's sermons that boldly warned us about sin but spoke lovingly of God's love and grace.

Mother was at her best on summer Sundays when it was our turn to have Reverend and Sister Freeman at our house for supper after the service. As soon as we arrived home and made Reverend and Mrs. Freeman comfortable—before getting the already cooked food ready to serve, Mother excused herself to her room and reappeared with a broad smile on her face, wearing her special dress. We called it the "dancing dress," because when she wore it her steps took on a liveliness that closely resembled dancing.

The Dress

The neckline of the bodice was cut low, coming to rest on her shoulders and adorned with a six-inch deep ruffle made of rose-colored calico with tiny white flowers. The ruffle was edged with a band of orange calico with tiny darker orange dots. Just above it was a row of yellow rickrack. The skirt was made of alternating gores of yellow and white calico with the orange dotted fabric edging the bodice. Over the skirt was an apron made with patches of the rose calico, a purple and yellow print, and a green and rose print. The apron was trimmed to match the ruffles at the neckline. A rose satin ribbon tied in a bow with a silk flower in the center was sewn onto the front center of the apron's waistband. The dress was that of a happy young girl who had no reason to doubt any of the promises upon which her joy rested. I wanted to know if this dress had always belonged to her. And if so, when did everything change? But I decided not to ask.

After the company had left on these special Sundays and Father was taking his walk around the fields and pastures, Mother always called us to the cool east side of the house by the chimney to read Bible stories to us. She sat on a folding chair with Florence, Sammy, and me sitting on the grass at her feet. Even after we had learned to read and knew most of the stories, we had no desire to miss hearing them again and experiencing the joy of her presence.

It was on one of those occasions that I found the courage to ask her where the dress came from.

Mother spoke excitedly at first, telling us about a special trip to a store to buy fabric for a celebration and how her mother had mixed together all the different colored pieces. When she reached the apron and the shoulder ruffles, she hesitated. Then, while rubbing her hands gently across the ruffles and the squares in the apron, the energy left her

27

voice, except for enough to say, "This one belonged to my sister."

All of us stared at Mother open-mouthed for a moment, then at each other. I blurted out, "You have a sister? We have an aunt?" I pictured a beautiful, happy woman who looked like Mother with dimples and puffy, cottony, soft hair, excitedly opening her arms at the first sight of me, eager to pull me in close to her and...

"No," Mother spoke almost in a whisper. "She is gone." Then she became silent, and her stare became distant. Knowing that she was no longer present with us, we arose and left her to her silence.

Mother continued to wear her dress on those Sundays, even though the spell appeared to have been broken. We continued to come with her to hear the stories, but we never again asked her about the dress.

The Last Watering

A FTER THE GREENING of the cornfields and the gardens, the rains became more and more sparse, then stopped altogether. I still held out hope that when the zinnias were tall and blooming Father would appear and take Mother by the hand and lead her into the garden as he always had, wading knee high and Mother wading almost to her waist in the sea of rainbow colors. But the zinnias struggled, attempting to make use of the morning dew when there was no longer any rain. They appeared to be renewed and thriving at sunrise, but by evening the plumpness was gone from their leaves, leaving them hanging limply on weakening stems. They were only half as tall as they should have been, their tiny buds struggling to grow into full blossoms.

I thought the zinnias could endure anything. But Father always said, pointing his finger to emphasize each word, as he did when he felt deeply about what he was saying, "When any plant has been deprived of what it needs over and over again, after a while parts of it will start to die, and

"Always refill the pail with the first stream of water so that you don't forget to set aside some water to prime the pump the next time you need water," he warned. "This one works just like the other one," he continued. "You have to first put water in it to get the water out. What does this pump teach us about life?" he then asked with a smile.

Florence answered, "It teaches us to think about the future, not just the present. If you just think about getting the water you need now and forget to fill the priming pail, you can't get water the next time."

"That's right," Father responded with obvious pride. "What does it teach you, Sammy?"

"To think about others," Sammy replied, punctuating his statement with a confident nod of his head. Father nodded back with a smile.

"And you, Hon?"

I was nervous about my answer because I knew that wasn't what everyone else was talking about, but it's what I felt, so I said, "I'm thinking that sooner or later a person is going to make a mistake and forget to prime the pump. So this teaches me about how blessed we are when there's someone who'll understand and who will not hold it against us and give us some water to start over again." My voice trailed off into a nervous whisper. Father studied my face for a moment, looked down and thought for a moment, then looked into my eyes and said, "Amen."

As I watered the zinnias, I knew it might be too late for them to become the beautiful sea of color they promised to be in the beginning. But after three days of watching their leaves turn bright green again and the side stems no longer drooping downward as they clung to the thicker and stronger main stems, I began to feel some hope that there would be enough blossoms to cheer Mother.

I started to fill my pail for the fourth watering and set it aside. As I pumped the handle, I marveled again at the cool stream of water that flowed so abundantly into the watering pail while the earth above was so dry and lifeless. When I started toward the garden, the pail swung like a pendulum with each of my steps, bumping the side of my leg, each swing causing the precious water to splash onto the hem of my dress, down the side of my legs, then flow down to my ankle to the ground before it got to the garden. To conserve each precious drop, I gathered up the other side of my dress and pulled it away from the pail and slowed my pace, holding the pail as steadily as I could.

I reached the first row and started to pour the water just around the root of each individual plant, being careful not to let any water spill into places where there were no zinnias. I was almost at the end of the first row when I heard the sound of footsteps on the dry, crackling grass. I looked up and saw Sammy.

There was something about Sammy's approach that caused my heart to sink. His walk was no longer his familiar walk. It was the walk of a would-be man. He walked with deliberation unlike anytime before, taking longer steps, planting each step firmly on the dry grass as if they were larger and heavier than they really were. He stopped just inside the garden, straightened his stance as if to elongate his body, and looked me in the eye. I noticed that his mischievous grin was gone. With a voice pitched lower than usual, he spoke.

"Some people's wells are getting low and some may even go dry, so we've got to save the water for us and for the vegetables. You should water the vegetables."

I hadn't thought about the vegetables for the past few days, or the corn or Sammy or anything else. Above all, I hadn't noticed that the Sammy I knew, who used to wait with me among the zinnias for the butterflies to come, was gone.

I thought Mother's garden would always be there. Even when Sammy, Florence, and I grew up it would be a place to which we could return and remember the best days. I thought that together we were ourselves a garden, with our roots firmly planted here even after life had called each of us elsewhere.

Mother was the yellow rose in the center of our garden, set apart from the others by the stone path encircling her, a plant around which air must flow freely and whose delicate, fragrant blossoms had to be approached with caution.

Florence was a glorious patch of black-eyed Susans, appearing each year larger than before; a patch of bright, gold flowers growing freely with parts of it appearing in unexpected places each year. She boldly claimed her space early in the spring and commanded attention with her brightness.

Sammy was a meadow sage with blazing purple spikes announcing his presence early in the season. He demanded little space and bloomed over and over, oblivious to the midday heat of the summer sun.

I was a morning glory whose vines reached for the sky but who needed something tall to which to cling. My blossoms opened in the safety of the cool, dewy morning and in the evening shade, but closed when the hot sun appeared. I wanted to be like the zinnia that stood bold and strong, defying the sun.

Our garden was enclosed by four tall cedars, one each on the north, south, east, and west corners, protecting us from the coldest and hottest dry winds and defining us as a garden. I thought Father was that hedge of cedars.

I thought the sun was always faithful in giving life. It rose and set so faithfully that I knew it was there even when the clouds covered it. But it had proven to be ruthless in its shining, not relenting either for the strong or the weak. It even appeared that Father and the sun had conspired to take everything away from us, especially Mother.

A Prayer for the Rain Dance

A S I LAY in my bed that night, unwilling to give up hope, I remembered a story Mother had told us about a prophet named Elijah whom God sent out to demonstrate to His people, Israel, that He was the one true God so that their hearts would turn back to Him and away from the false gods that they were worshiping. Elijah prophesied that there would be a drought—that there would be neither dew nor rain except by his word. Under God's direction, Elijah ordered a sacrifice on a mountain where there would be a contest to demonstrate God's glory and the uselessness of worshipping the powerless false gods.

Elijah prayed to God for it to be known that He was God of Israel and that Elijah was His servant following God's command. He prayed for God to answer him so that the people would know that the Lord was God and that He was turning their hearts back again.

Elijah prayed for the Lord to put His glory on display for the sake of His people, and in order to let them see that He was working to restore their faith. And God did. After the people had witnessed God's power, and their hearts were turned back to Him, a cloud the size of a man's hand appeared, and soon after that the rain poured.

That's when I got the idea to pray. So I quietly eased out of bed to keep from waking Florence and got on my knees on my side of the bed and began to whisper.

Dear God, I know you know everything. And I know you are in control of everything. You tell the snow when to fall and also the rain. And you commanded the rain to fall when your people, Israel, turned their hearts back to you. I don't know where Mother's heart is, but you do. And I'm asking you to show her your power to give her hope. I'm asking you to end the drought and bring Father back. But if you're not ready to end the drought, or it's not the time for Father to return, to still remember Mother by sending her some rain for her garden. I know that all you have to do is say "Let there be," and the rain will appear wherever you command it.

So tomorrow, when the sun poses itself in the sky to begin its reign of destruction, let a cloud about the size of a man's hand, like the one Elijah saw, appear over the western horizon. Then let me see the shadow of the cloud float over the dry ground as it approaches our house. Let the cloud grow larger and darker as it slowly moves toward our house obscuring the blinding brightness of the sun. Let me hear the rumble of thunder and see flashes of lightning dance across the sky. Let the tall oak tree sway in the rumbling wind. Let the boards on the barn creak and the loose tin on the barn roof beat like drums while the cloud hovers over our house and Mother's garden. Let me hear a single drop of rain tap on my dusty window pane then trickle down, making a clear streak in its path. Let the drops fall faster with the thundering sound of stampeding hooves. Let the rain flow down Mother's window in sheets, washing away all the dust and despair.

Let me see Mother enter her garden and prance toward the center with the swaying hem of her dancing dress brushing the tops of the once-dying zinnias. Let steam rise from the ground as the cool rain falls on the hot, dry grass. And let its crackling sounds be silent under her feet. Let the drooping leaves of the zinnias begin to swell with the water flowing so abundantly over them. Let the newly drenched stems and unopened blossom heads stand upright as they are filled with new life.

Let the water flow into the cracks of the parched earth, then overflow into streams, rushing to the ends of the rows. Let Mother's dress become heavy with the weight of the water flowing downward and dripping off its hem onto the ground around her feet. Let me see her standing at the center of her garden with her face tilted heavenward as the water forms sheets of glaze over her skin as it flows into the corners of her eyes, down her cheeks, and into her hair. Let the water splash off her palms as they are lifted up in praise to you.

If you are not ready to end the drought everywhere, Lord, just send Mother her own patch of rain for her sake to let her know that you are working to restore her.

But the next day, a Saturday, there was no rain. Instead, the sun started its reign early by taking away the dew. It seemed to shine more angrily than before, with a fiery glow that sent torrents of heat. Hot winds blew over the dirt road in front of the house, lifting the sand off the road, sweeping up a cloud of dust and sending it across the browning cornfield, whipping across Mother's garden and snatching the clinging life out of the leaves, buds, and stems of her zinnias.

Just after sunset that day, as I watered the vegetables, I heard the voices of Reverend and Mrs. Freeman at the front door. Reverend Freeman's voice held the familiar compassion unexpected in a voice as deep and strong as his. Mrs. Freeman's voice was sweet and kind as usual. As time passed, Mother's voice became more and more cheerful as they sat on the front porch.

Although I would like to have lingered in their presence for a while, I stayed in the garden until they left, for fear that I might give away my secret, because I had resolved never to tell anyone about my silly prayer.

C h a p t e r   N i n e

The Living Water

W HEN I WENT inside after Reverend and Mrs.
Freeman left, I found Mother in the kitchen with
Florence. Mother seemed to be in charge again.

"Go get Sammy, Hon," she commanded softly.

I did, and I returned with Sammy who wore a puzzled
look on his face. I didn't remember what anyone talked
about except that Mother told us to get everything ready
for church the next day. And I remember how her eyes held
a degree of hope and anticipation that I had not witnessed
all summer.

The next morning, we set out for church. We stepped
off the side porch and onto the driveway where Father's car,
which had not been driven all summer, was parked. None
of us asked why Mother chose to walk. We simply followed
her. She moved with a sense of purpose that one has when
on an important quest.

We started down the dusty road Father had traveled
when he left. This led us to a narrow, shady, northbound
lane that connected to the highway that lead us to Mount

Carmel, our church. Sammy walked beside Mother with Florence and me behind. The tail of Mother's yellow and blue floral-print dress swayed slightly with each step. Her purse swung like a pendulum on her arm. Her blue, flower-adorned hat reminded me of the Sundays we had enjoyed before. This gave me a surge of anticipation. Sammy wore his dark Sunday suit that Mother had let down the night before to accommodate his growth over the summer.

As we stepped onto the shoulder of the paved highway and headed toward the church, the midmorning sun blazed triumphantly behind us, it's heat rising from the concrete highway. On the shoulder of the highway we walked over patches of dry grass alternating with patches of bare ground sprinkled with tiny rocks. Florence tipped daintily to protect her high heels. Her hips swayed in her white eyelet sundress with the pink, purple, and yellow flowers embroidered at the hem, as she anticipated the conquests she'd enjoy as the boys clamored for her attention. I walked beside her in my yellow dress with the long sash.

My face was beginning to perspire by the time we came to the little stores built of weathering wood with brightly colored metal signs nailed to the front walls and hanging in the windows. I knew then that we were near the small church with the white steeple that would welcome us.

As we got closer, I could see the brothers and sisters standing under the portico. Others stood outside under the large oak tree that stood tall and unwilted and untouched by the drought.

The men, who usually stood strong and straight in their pressed suits and crisp white shirts with their legs slightly spread and their hands clasped behind them with their eyes focused intently upon the person to whom they were talking, seemed tired. They sat on the steps or leaned against the tree, rising only to shake hands and give welcoming hugs. They talked about just one thing—the drought. As we drew closer, their talk gave way to welcoming greetings as the attention turned to us.

"We've been worried about you, Sister Clara. It's so good to see you back with us," Brother Frank spoke, reaching out his hand to shake each one of ours.

"Praise the Lord, Sister. Give me a big hug!" cried Sister Jones, as she reached out to hug each one of us.

Sammy, Florence, and I tore away at the first opportunity to join the young people on the last remaining patch of grass under another oak tree on the east side of the church.

Boys darted about, some with their Easter suits still hanging loosely to leave room for another year's growth. Girls Florence's age passed conspicuously by them to show off their freshly done hair and their gathered dresses flaring out from their slender waists, playing hide-and-seek with their eyes as proud fathers kept a watchful eye on them.

The bell rang, summoning us all into the church. I sat in the pew across from Mother, where I could still be close to the young ones who felt too grown up to sit with their mothers and fathers, but where I could still see the side of her face.

After the deacons led us in hymns and prayed on their knees by the table up front, Reverend Freeman rose from his kingly chair on the left side of the pulpit and moved to the lectern in the center. There was something comforting about the round fullness of his face and the soft, round bulge of his stomach shaping the drapes of his long, black robe. He raised his hands to signal us to stand, causing the full sleeves of his robe to fan out into what I called angel wings.

His voice was rich and strong but kind and compassionate, the way it was when he visited Mother. As he began speaking to us, his eyes scanned the congregation, making contact with each of us. His voice was like that of a father speaking to a despondent child.

"I know most of you have a heavy heart today, some heavier than others," he began. "Some of you may feel forsaken by God, even afraid. Some of you may feel as if the Lord has been holding back His blessings from you this summer. I know you've been saying among yourselves, 'If the rain doesn't come soon, everything is going to be lost.' You may doubt God's love for you right now. You might even be wondering, *What did I do to cause God to punish me like this?*" Then, after a pause, he added, with his voice mirroring the doubt and confusion in the hearts of many, "Some of you may even be asking yourselves or each other, *What kind of God would let something like this happen?*

"But through all of this, I don't want any of you to forget what you know about our wonderful Father," he gently admonished. Then, leaning forward over the lectern, silently scanning the congregation, he spoke again in a loud, yet still-gentle voice, "Let me remind you of what kind of God we have. Better still; let us see what His Word tells us.

"Let us start with number one. Genesis 1:1 tells us that in the beginning God created the heavens and the earth. So our God is the Creator. And you also remember that over and over, during the six days of creation, God gave approval of His work with the statement that it was good. There were no droughts, no famines, and no death. Everything was good."

I missed some of what Reverend Freeman said next as I tried to imagine what things were like with everything being perfect. I marveled at the fact that things had ever been perfect. I knew that the first sin caused all types of troubles, but I hadn't really thought about how perfect everything was before sin came into the world. It seemed as though there had always been trouble.

Anyway, Reverend Freeman got my attention again when he straightened up and began to speak louder and faster, as if he were bursting with excitement over some good news that he was eager to share. Then, with two fingers pointing upward and briskly waving his hand from side to side, he continued.

"Number two is so important for us to remember when we are questioning God's love. We don't always understand His ways, but we can always be sure of His love. And that's what number two is. We have a God of love."

What he said next helped me to understand how God's love can be with us even when bad things are happening.

"Knowing the sinful condition that we are in, God could have just turned His back on us and left us without any hope. And that means all of us, for Romans 3:23 tells us that all have sinned and fall short of the glory of God. But God promised to send someone to save us by paying the price for our sins so that we could still be His children and have a loving relationship with Him now and forever. Since we couldn't do this by ourselves, He gave His only begotten son, Jesus Christ, who died on the cross to take away the sins of those who believe in Him as Savior. So when you have doubt, remember the everlasting love stated in John 3:16, which tells us that He gave His Son for us.

The passage that he read next really touched my heart:

> For I am persuaded that neither death nor life, nor angels nor principalities nor powers, nor things present nor things to come, nor height nor depth, nor any other created thing, shall be able to separate us from the love of God which is in Christ Jesus our Lord.
> —Romans 8: 38-39

Then he told us that God will never leave us alone in our suffering. And the next two passages seemed to have been chosen just for Sammy, Florence, Mother, and me as he read them to us:

When my father and my mother forsake me, Then the Lord will take care of me.

—Psalm 27:10

For He Himself has said, "I will never leave you nor forsake you."

—Hebrews 13:5b

It felt good to be reminded that everything we do and everything that happens to us is covered under God's love.

"Our God also gives His hope in His promises to restore everything," Reverend Freeman continued. "So number three is that our God is the God of restoration. Scripture promises us that Christ is going to return and that all of creation groans for His return. We are promised that when He returns, all things in the heavens and on earth will be made new and perfect again."

When he said that, I pictured all of us back together again, with the pastures and cornfields green and the zinnias blazing with color.

After a pause followed by a sigh, he continued, "God is constantly restoring us—those of us who are believers in Jesus Christ as our Savior." And he recited passages that speak about this restoration and renewal.

He restores my soul.

—Psalm 23:3a

Create in me a pure heart, O God, and renew a steadfast spirit within me.

—Psalm 51:10.

Restore in me the joy of Your salvation, and uphold me by Your generous Spirit.

—Psalm 51:12

But those who wait upon the Lord shall renew their
strength; They shall mount up with wings like eagles,
They shall run and not be weary, They shall walk and
not faint.

—Isaiah 40:31a

"Number four," he continued, "we have a God who is in
control of everything. And He has an eternal plan and a purpose
for everything that He brings into our lives, with the ultimate
goal being our salvation. And that plan was in place for each of
us individually before we were born. We see this demonstrated
in the book of Jeremiah when God called Jeremiah to be His
prophet." Then he read to us the scripture:

Before I formed you in the womb I knew you;
Before you were born I sanctified you;
I ordained you a prophet to the nations.

—Jeremiah 1:5

"So everything that has already happened, that's happening now, and that will happen in the future is to serve
His purposes. Romans 8:28 assures us that in all things God
works for the good of those who love Him and are called
according to His purposes, so that ultimately we may be in
the host of believers when Christ returns.

"I won't try to explain all the spiritual benefits of
suffering. But you'll recognize them as they come. He will
send the rain in His time and according to His love, mercy,
and wisdom.

"Because, number five, He is our provider. Matthew
6:25-26 reminds us not to worry about life, what we will
eat or what we will drink; nor about our bodies, what we
will put on; that the birds in the air neither sow nor reap
nor gather into barns. Yet our heavenly Father feeds them.

We are reminded that we are more than they. And Jeremiah
29:11 tells us that God's plans are to prosper us and not
harm us, to give us hope and a future. But in the meantime,
He wants to rain down His Holy Spirit upon us." Then he
shared with us God's promises to Israel.

> For I will pour water on him who is thirsty,
> And floods on the dry ground;
> I will pour My Spirit on your descendants,
> And My blessing on your offspring
> They will spring up among the grass
> Like willows by the watercourses.
> —Isaiah 44:3-4

And what Christ himself promises to us now:

> If anyone thirsts, let him come to Me and drink.
> He who believes in Me, as the Scripture has said,
> out of his heart will flow rivers of living water.
> —John 7:37-38

"And finally, number six," Reverend Freeman said, "we
have a God who is faithful. So whatever He promises you
can be sure He will deliver. He promised us a Savior and
kept that promise in John 3:16. And 1 Corinthians 15:3-4
tells us that the promises in scripture were realized when
Christ died, was buried and rose again on the third day.
So let us be joyful in the midst of our troubles as we look
forward to His promises unfolding in our lives. And, in
the meantime, while we wait on the Lord, let us continue
to worship together, let us comfort and show love to one
another. Let us forgive as we have been forgiven.

"These are just a few of the attributes of our God. But
for today, I must come to a close with the reading of three
final passages." And he read to us these passages.

Blessed is the man who trusts in the Lord,
And whose hope is in the Lord.
For he shall be like a tree planted by the waters,
Which spreads out its roots by the river,
And will not fear when heat comes;
But its leaf will be green,
And will not be anxious in the year of drought,
Nor will cease from yielding fruit.

—Jeremiah 17:7-8

Be anxious for nothing, but in everything by prayer and
supplication, with thanksgiving, let your request be made
known to God; and the peace of God, which surpasses
all understanding, will guard your hearts and minds
through Christ Jesus.

—Philippians 4:6-7

Peace I leave with you. My peace I give to you; not as
the world gives do I give to you. Let not your heart be
troubled, neither let it be afraid.

—John 14:27

A thunder of amens erupted when Reverend Freeman
finished. As I looked around me, I saw tears flowing in tiny
streams from the eyes of the sisters and the brothers. Feet
tapped like the sounds of stampeding raindrops, while the
flutter stirred the stagnant air.

The piano keys rang out like the crystal sound of rushing
water. The choir then rose in a mass of cloudy black robes and
began to sway like wind-blown trees and began to sing:

"I shall not be I shall not be moved
I shall not be I shall not be moved
Just like a tree planted by the wa-ter..."

Faint whimpers came from the grownup side. Dainty lace handkerchiefs and large, thick cotton squares mopped trickles of water from the eyes of the men and women whose hearts had found peace.

I looked over at Mother and saw her lift her face and her palms heavenward. I saw her lips whisper, "Yes, Jesus."

On the walk home, Mother's pace was fast, and she held her head high and her shoulders straight. The sun hung defeated in the sky, stripped of its power to harm us. I knew it wasn't the music or the salty tears that gave this new energy to Mother. It was God's Word and the Living Water—the Holy Spirit—that filled her with new life.

When we reached home, Mother went straight to the zinnias that stood like skeletons in straight lines along the tops of the rows. With her purse still hanging on her arm, her Sunday shoes still on her feet, and the blue silk-flowered hat still on her head, with her free hand she started to yank out the dead stems one by one until all of them were uprooted and tossed onto a pile at the southwest corner of the garden. While Sammy and Florence had rushed inside to change out of their Sunday clothes, I sat on the steps and watched her. I did not offer to help her nor speak. I sensed that she needed to do this alone.

It wasn't until she was completely finished that she straightened her body and took a deep breath and looked at me and spoke.

"Tell Florence and Sammy to come here." Her voice was commanding but gentle. "I want all of you to come with me to the side of the house. I have something to tell you."

On our way there I glanced back at the pile of stiff, lifeless zinnias and decided that I didn't want to be the zinnia in our garden after all. I wanted to be something more deeply rooted.

Chapter Ten

Mother's Story

WHEN I BROUGHT Florence and Sammy out of the house, Mother was already seated in her chair. A breeze magnified the cooling effect of the shade as we took our places at her feet.

"I want to tell you all the story of the dress," she began. She sighed deeply and continued.

"I grew up in a place that I've never told you about. It's where I met and married your father before we came to live with Grandpa. Our land was hilly with sandy red soil. Pine and oak trees grew along the slopes. Histories of past rains were etched in zigzag patterns down the sides of the hills where rainwater rushed downward exposing the roots of small pine trees that were clinging tenaciously to the remaining earth.

"Father loved the trees," she said.

"'Almost everything in nature depends on a tree in some way,' he would say with firm conviction, punctuating each word with a point of his finger. 'They're the biggest form of plant life, but can be destroyed by something as small as

49

beetle larvae. As big as it is, it needs water. If anything big or small gets into it and eats away or destroys the channel by which the water gets to its branches, it dies.'"

Mother continued, "In the autumn, when there was open land, cotton boles turned soft, sunny, rolling hills and plateaus into a blinding whiteness, while soft, brown, drying cornstalks rustled in the crisp breeze.

"A winding road led from a busy, distant highway to our house and community in the woods. Our house looked like all the other houses in our little community. It nestled on a plateau of one of the softer hills. Built of wood that had weathered to a serene gray, it looked as natural there as the birds' nests, or as if it could have grown there along with the big oak tree that stood on the west side. Except for the shade of the oak tree, our house stood sun-drenched above the smaller trees that dotted the land around it. My mother had a zinnia garden growing in the front yard just beyond the porch, and from that garden, bouquets were cut to adorn the church on summer Sundays.

"The earth yielded neither freely nor abundantly, but the harshness of farm life was balanced by the caring among the people. The strength of our community was Canaan, our little church built on the harvest tithing of its fifty families. Father was a deacon there, and Mother was a small, happy woman who served joyfully whenever she was asked to serve. Father was kind to everyone at church, but he was stern at home. He demanded perfection from all of us, but his sternness was balanced by Mother's gentleness.

"Sharing was a way of life. Families who were experts in or had the best soil for growing a certain crop shared with those who were less fortunate. Families with sons sent their sons to help families who had none with heavier tasks. Families with daughters sent their daughters to help families who had none with domestic chores such as canning.

"Minnie and I jumped rope together under the oak tree whenever we had free time. As little girls we played among the smiling faces of our church family on Sunday mornings before the bell rang for us to go inside. When we grew older we danced among the winking eyes of boys with bumpy faces and cracking voices. Minnie giggled and hid her face when I teased her at home about the attention she and Reverend Harris's son paid each other.

"The last time I saw Minnie, she was 16 and I was 15. Although I was a year younger, we were the same size and height. We had abandoned our jump ropes in favor of scouting the church grounds on Sunday mornings and at church festivals for the cutest and best dressed boys, although Minnie and the pastor's son had begun to head straight for each other every chance they got.

"Minnie and I had been looking forward to the Harvest Festival, when everyone would bring their harvest tithing to be shared with those in need and to be sold at the market place to support the church. We had picked the cloth for our dresses early that spring. I can picture even now the colorful display of the bolts of fabric lying on tables extending from one end to the other of a long room in a building with walls of unpainted lumber. I remember the sound of our feet walking across the wooden floor seeming to echo off the walls as we moved excitedly from aisle to aisle.

"When we both reached for the same orange and yellow fabrics, Mother came over to mediate before a dispute emerged. 'Why don't you pick another fabric to go with this one, and I'll mix the two together so that both of you can have the same fabrics. I'll just make the matching shoulder ruffle and apron different on each dress.' She always said, 'There is no reason why a lady shouldn't still look dressed up in the kitchen.' So she did make the aprons and match them with the shoulder ruffles. One was made in shades of orange and yellow, and the other one is the dress that I wear.

"But a drought came that summer just like the one we're having now," she continued. "And without a harvest, many of the families were destined to lose their land. Even our church, which held us all together, stood to perish. Just like now, so much depended on the rain. Father grew angry, and Mother was on her knees praying more than we'd ever seen her pray."

"'What kind of God would let something like this happen?' became Father's song whether he was in the dying fields, on the porch, under the oak tree, or at the dinner table. Mother always responded with God's promises. 'The righteous will not go hungry,' she'd say.

"As the days and weeks went by, Father's voice became louder and louder behind the closed doors of their bedroom at night, overpowering Mother's soft plea for him to have faith. By the middle of the summer, when hope was dwindling, evenings that Minnie and I once spent watching fireflies and listening to frogs and crickets outside our window were given over to listening in silent fear to Father's roaring voice.

"One night, as we listened for the voices, Mother stormed out of their room toward the kitchen. Minnie and I ran after her. But avoiding looking us in the eye, in a soft, tired voice, she said, 'Go back to your room, I'm all right.'

"Minnie wasn't afraid to be angry, so the wide-eyed fear in her eyes turned to squinting anger. And after we went to bed she tossed and turned far into the night.

"I tried to be extra nice to Mother the next day, but Father's anger took charge again. At supper, as we ate in intense silence, that silence was suddenly broken when he pounded his fist on the table and exclaimed, 'How could God let something like this happen!' We all jumped as the plates, knives, forks, and spoons flew up from the table, some landing on the wood floor with clinking sounds. Mother jumped, then remained silent and still. Again, Minnie's eyes became two barely open but piercing slits focused on Father. Seeming to calm down, he arose and stormed out into the darkness.

"Minnie and I were still awake when Father returned. We heard Mother's soft voice welcome him and his gruff reply. His voice became louder and louder until finally Mother rushed to the kitchen again. This time, as we rushed after her, she broke into tears. 'I give up,' she cried.

"Minnie bolted into their room where Father was. Mother and I turned and rushed after her. With the force of someone much larger than she, Mother flung Minnie aside as Father looked up from his large, tattered leather chair. I hadn't noticed until then how rounded his shoulders had become. He seemed paralyzed in that position as he looked up at the scene in front of him with disbelief in his eyes. Mother held Minnie in her arms until she stopped struggling. Once free, she glared at Father. And with tears running down her face, she hissed, "You hypocrite! You hypocrite! You call yourself a deacon? You stand up there in front of everybody every Sunday and pretend. Well, I'm going to be standing up there Sunday, and I'm telling everybody you're just a hypocrite! I'm going to tell them everything!'

When Minnie rushed past me toward our room, I followed her. I found her sitting on the edge of the bed, staring blankly across the room, her hands shaking.

"'Some part of me that I didn't know was there took charge without my permission—without any warning. And before I knew it, I was in there standing in front of Father, screaming and wanting to do even more than that,' she whispered, looking down at her hands as if she were seeing them for the first time.

"We ate breakfast in silence the next morning. The silence and the way Father and Mother avoided looking at Minnie and me spoke of something we were all feeling—that nothing would be the same again. Something had been shattered into pieces so small that it seemed impossible to find them all and put them back together again. Some were lost in the cracks of the graying wood floor of our house; some flew away with the dust on the wind that swept across the dirt road.

"I was relieved to hear the faint sound coming from Mother's direction. We all looked her way, hoping perhaps for something healing to fall from her lips. But still looking down at her plate she simply spoke softly.

"'Mr. McGee's sister over in Riverton is still sick. In fact, he said she's getting worse. And he can no longer make that five-hour trip one way to check on her every week. So he's looking for someone to move in with her so that she'll have someone to look after her every day.' Then, looking softly at Minnie, she said, 'He thinks the world of you, Minnie, and he thinks you'd be the perfect person for the job. And I think so, too. He's been asking if you could go, and I think you should.'

"'Yes, ma'am,' Minnie responded without hesitation.

"Father's hands were relaxed and still then. And they were steady as he reached for a warm biscuit, separated the top from the bottom, placed a lump of butter on the bottom piece with his knife and put the two parts back together in four easy steps. He was himself again. Someone had paid. At that moment, I thought about sacrifices—how sometimes one person can give up or lose so much and the difference it can make for everybody else. And I marveled at how sweetly Minnie gave up everything.

"A brother from the church came for Minnie in a buggy with bright red wheels and a soft-looking red leather cushion on the seat. He said Mr. McGee had sent him. Except for my heavy heart, everything about me was numb as I watched her take up her bags that lay on our bed.

"I took one of her bags and she took the other as we went out to the buggy together. Before she climbed onto the buggy seat, we hugged. Then Minnie gave me a smile and a mischievous wink and said, 'Take care of your new dress.' I stood and watched until the buggy disappeared around the winding curve. When I turned to go inside, I found Mother standing expressionless just outside the door. At that moment, I lost my sister, and I decided that I had lost my mother too.

"We didn't lose our land after all, and none of our neighbors had to leave our community. We just shared our farm with another family at our church. All the families agreed that instead of all of us losing our land, we would pool our money and pay off as many of the farms as we could, choosing the ones centered nearest to the church.

"The rains came too late for a harvest, but everyone agreed to meet on the day of the Harvest Festival anyway to give thanks for our many blessings, despite the drought. Mother and Father let me stay home that day. And although I wasn't going to wear it, I decided to open the trunk where Minnie and I had stored our dresses. I wanted to look at my dress to remember her. When I looked inside, I understood the secret behind her wink when she told me to take care of my dress. My heart came alive again when I found that she had taken my dress and left me hers. So the dress you've seen me wear is hers.

"A new boy came to work in our community to help build homes and barns on the newly-divided land the following spring. He was your father. A year later we were married and moved in with your Grandpa.

When she had finished speaking, we all just looked down until Sammy asked, "Where is she now?"

"I don't know," Mother answered. "I didn't want to speak to Mother and Father about her anymore. And nobody else talked about her either. So there was no one that I could ask to help me. I was still young when I left with your father. So I had no idea were Riverton was. I had never been away from home, so I didn't know how to get anywhere. I thought maybe Minnie would come looking for me after she was done there. I always thought she was so much stronger and braver than I was. After many years, I just gave up. I guess I was hurt even more that she didn't come and find me."

"Father would have helped," Florence stated with certainty.

"I was so angry and hurt that I could never talk about it. So he doesn't even know I have a sister because she was gone and everybody was silent about it by the time he came to our community."

I understood a lot that I couldn't express. All I could think to say was, "I like it when you wear that dress Mother."

It was good just to sit with her for a while with none of us feeling as if we needed to say anything. Mother's voice had sounded stronger than it did the first time she tried to tell us about the dress, and she had smiled a few times as she told us about her and Minnie together.

When I was confident that she was all right, I stood up and said, 'Thank you, Mother." Then I asked, "Should I water the vegetables?"

"Yes, Hon," she replied. "And I'll help."

Chapter Eleven

Watering With Mother

MOTHER STOOD UP. As I looked up at her, her gaze was gentle and loving. I was at that moment a child again, with the ground once more feeling solid underneath my feet. A smile blossomed as she said, "You see, Hon, there've been droughts before."

When we reached the pump, I picked up the priming pail and pumped the water into it. Remembering what Father told us, I held the priming pail under the spout with my right hand to refill it and reached for the pump handle with my left hand. I felt Mother's soft hand gently lift mine from the handle as she spoke, "I pump, and you hold the pail."

As we began to fill the pail for the garden, we agreed on an alternate plan. I would pump and she'd water; then she pumped and I'd water the next time. She could have sent me for another pail, but we chose to share the one between us.

The vegetables had survived due to the watering that I had done. And from that day on, Mother and I watered together. We knew each plant well and marveled together at every inch of new growth and every vegetable we harvested.

Our watering ritual ended just before the end of summer when the first rain came in the night while we slept. The rain continued the next day accompanied by loud thunder and bright flashes of lightening.

After the storm, Mother and I sat on the side porch in rocking chairs, each of us holding a large, white-enameled metal pan with a red stripe running around the top rim. They were identical except that mine had a chip where the side curved into the bottom, exposing the metal layer underneath. Each pan was filled with crisp and succulent snap beans ready to be snapped and strung.

Mother marveled at how cool and misty the air was, how the leaves of the trees had plumped up, and how enough rain had come that there was still water standing in the ditches and in the lower fields at the far end of the farm where some corn had survived the drought.

"What good is the rain now?" I asked her, feeling indignant about the irony of it all.

"Well," she responded, "the more rain the earth receives even now, the deeper the moisture will go into the soil. And the deeper the moisture, the deeper the roots of the trees and some of the other plants will grow. And the deeper the roots grow, the better they will be prepared if another drought comes next summer. Even some of the plants that come back each year will survive the winter better if the soil is moist."

"Is that how the Living Water works in us, too?" I asked, before I had time to think about the question too long and change my mind. "Is that why you're better?"

"Yes," she answered.

Chapter Twelve

The Winter

WE CONTINUED TO meet on the side of the house each Sunday afternoon. When Sammy and Florence were gone, Mother and I still met. She started asking me to tell or read stories too.

Sammy and Florence were home more on Sundays during the winter, so Mother prompted them to tell or read stories as well. We sat in her room with her, the warm fire glowing in the fireplace, and the bright colors of the quilts and fabrics made each gathering a special privilege.

During those times with her, seeing how different she was, I realized that if God had sent the rain onto her garden last summer, she would not have been ready for it, and it might not have helped, because that wasn't the kind of water she needed.

My favorite story was one that Florence read to us about Ruth. I liked it at first because of the love stories. But when she read it again, and Mother helped her explain it more deeply, I saw even more. I saw the parts about famine and plenty; spiritual emptiness and spiritual food; feeling abandoned by God and receiving His presence and His blessings; spiritual and earthly loss and restoration; and even a picture of God's love and redemption through Christ. And when Sammy told the story of Samson and his strength again, I realized for the first time that his strength was not in his hair, but in his relationship with God.

A rare snow came that winter. Large, fluffy flakes floated on the cold air, then fell to the ground, covering the brown winter grass and the places where the summer flowers never grew and turning the yard and fields into what seemed like a fantasy with unimaginable flawlessness.

Unlike the stampeding late summer rain, the snow fell silently. And unlike summer flowers, which simply make things that surround us seem more pleasant, for a while the snow covered everything in a blanket of purity and perfection. With both, our pretenses have to eventually give way to what is true and lasting.

The snow became thicker and thicker until I could barely see the road from the door on the side porch. For a moment, I thought I saw Father approaching our house. I became frustrated that I couldn't recognize his gait even though he was far away and obscured by the snow. I felt that I should have known with certainty whether it was he or not. *Just one summer shouldn't be enough to erase my memory of his walk!* I thought.

I watched from inside the glass door that replaced the summer screen door protected from the cold outside. As the tall figure came closer, I became more excited. But after what seemed like a brief pause where the driveway met the road, he moved on.

I moved quickly to the northeast window of the front room, hoping to get a closer glimpse of him as he continued past the house. I hoped to observe him more closely to find some proof in his walk that it was Father. When I saw his frame move from one side to the other, appearing to generate momentum with each swing of his long arms, just like Father, memories of him began to surge. But like my silly prayer, I could have been wrong again. So at the risk of being embarrassed, I decided not to tell anyone.

Whether it was Father I saw or not, it was still a beautiful winter. I enjoyed the pink and blue morning sky touching the ground beyond the leafless trees. And when the wind blew crystals of snow from the roof above Mother's window, I loved how they sparkled in the afternoon sunshine before being blown onto her windowpane for a last sparkling moment of glory before melting into a downward stream of water.

Chapter Thirteen

The Ritual

SPRING CAME AGAIN, coaxing tender green shoots to the top of the ground. The rains came as usual, loading the branches once stiffened by the winter's freeze with sparkling water droplets.

We went about our usual preparations for the summer with hope for an abundant autumn harvest. But Mother's zinnia garden lay untouched. Little attention was paid to the tiny weeds sprouting on the rows that had been almost flattened by time and the rains of last fall and the new spring. No one expressed any regrets that there were no seeds or that Father was not there to do the digging. We had all changed. We had learned things that we did not know before. Our greatest hopes no longer hung on the promises of spring or the sun or the rain—or anyone or anything on the earth. And I knew that Mother no longer needed the zinnias in the same way she needed them before. Maybe she didn't need Father in the same way either.

Still, I awoke each morning compelled to look through the side door facing the garden in case Father was out there with his shovel poised to turn the first clod of earth. Sometimes I even thought I heard the ringing sound of the hoe breaking up the clods.

Then, early one Saturday morning, I awoke to find him in the garden. He must have arrived at early dawn before we had awakened and when there was just enough light to see, for when I saw him, he was standing at the far edge of the garden with his shovel positioned to turn the last clump of soil.

I don't know what brought him back home. Maybe it was because spring was a good time to make a fresh start. Or maybe it was remembering all the springs past and longing to fall into the familiar rhythm of nature that seems to begin with spring. Or maybe this was the one place he could find without having to search. I was convinced, however, that more than anything else it was the language of the ritual that he needed to speak to Mother again.

I didn't hurry out the door to the steps this time, because I sensed that I didn't belong there. Instead, I went to Mother's room to wake her, but I found her already looking out her window from her sewing chair, her face devoid of emotion. She had watched him take up the hoe and go from row to row as he broke up the clods of dirt to form the rows of powdery soil. Although the sun had just risen and the spring air was still cool, sweat had begun to form in shining beads on his face and to seep from his chest and back onto his shirt. I don't know if he knew that Mother was watching, but he looked her way when the last row was done. He stood leaning on the handle of the hoe that he had positioned under his right arm and faced her window.

I thought of how he had left Mother without warning and left all of us to endure such a hard summer without him. I thought of how she had to face realities about him and everything else that she wasn't ready to face. And I thought of how the love we once had for someone can seem lost and irretrievable, requiring us to search for new reasons to love him or her again. But Mother didn't appear to waver. Maybe she credited Father with the sweat on his brow or the straightness of the rows. Or maybe it was something she knew about his heart that didn't match what he had done. And maybe it was knowing his heart that made her react as she did. Or maybe it was what Reverend Freeman said about forgiving as we have been forgiven. Whatever the reason, what happened next surprised me.

Mother arose from her chair. I followed her as she moved toward the side door leading onto the side porch. I stopped at the screen door and watched as she opened it and moved onto the porch under the arch of the climbing rose bush and down the steps into the garden. They stood silently facing each other for a moment. I don't know why, but I saw no anger in the way Mother stood. Instead, she reached for his hand and led him toward the door.

I moved to Florence's room and found her still sleeping. "Father's home," I announced excitedly.

"He is?" Before I could answer, she asked, "Does Sammy know?"

We found Sammy awake, lying face-up his bed with both palms supporting the back of his head.

"Do you know that Father's home?" Florence asked.

"Yeah," he said, then rolled over and lay silently with his back toward us.

"Let's cook Father a Sunday dinner and use the Sunday dishes," Florence suggested, her voice still filled with excitement.

That's just like Florence not to dwell on anything I thought, as I agreed. Sometimes she appeared not to care about serious things. But she had listened to that story Father told about the lost son. And she had listened to Reverend

Freeman. She acted as if there were nothing to forgive, and she chose to let Sammy feel however he wanted to feel.

There was an unspoken agreement between Florence and me that we wouldn't disturb Mother and Father. We knew Sammy wouldn't either. The harmony between Father's strong, heavy voice and Mother's soft voice was soothing to me all day. After a few hours with Father, I even heard Mother laugh.

Florence showed me how to make her favorite dishes that she had learned to cook over the past year. But I mostly helped with the peeling, chopping, and keeping the dishes washed. We forgot about breakfast in all the excitement, but we prepared a large noonday meal.

Florence sent me over to Uncle Willis's to get Sammy, where I found him playing baseball with Cousin Jimmy and their friends. He was poised to pitch the ball when I spoke to him.

"Father's home," I said again, as if Sammy didn't hear Florence and me before.

He held the ball suspended in the air for several seconds before he replied. "I know." He focused his attention on throwing the ball.

"Florence has made a big dinner for all of us," I begged.

"I'm not hungry," he shouted with glaring eyes.

"You mean Uncle Jacob is back and you don't want to see him?" Jimmy questioned. "Let's all go see him."

"Not now," Sammy spoke in a kinder voice.

"Well, tell him we'll see him later," Jimmy requested as Sammy turned to accompany me home.

Chapter Fourteen

Father's Story

WHEN SAMMY AND I arrived at the table, Mother, Father, and Florence were already seated. Father and Mother were both smiling. Father's smile was broader and Mother's more reserved, as if she were holding back until some perfect moment when she knew she could trust what was happening.

Sammy hesitated at first, then took his seat next to Father, his back turned slightly toward him. His face was still angry, as if Father were the lost son in the story that he told us and had appeared out of nowhere to claim what he didn't deserve. Sammy acted as if he himself were the faithful son.

Although none of us were exactly the same as we were before Father left, we were prepared to play our old roles for his sake, except for Sammy.

Although smiling, Father seemed to avoid looking into our eyes. But I refused to turn away until he looked at me.

"Hey," he said with the familiar kindness in his voice.

"Hey," I responded, remembering that before he left, a simple "hey" and a smile were all we needed to communicate our love for each other.

"This is a feast, Florence!" he exclaimed with surprise in his voice. "You've become a great cook!"

"Thanks," she replied with a girlish grin.

"And you, Sammy! I hear that you've done a great job as man of the house. Would you take over the responsibility of giving thanks?" he asked.

Sammy gave Father a questioning look before a reluctant smile escaped from his lips. After Sammy gave thanks and we all said our verses, including Father, we passed the food around and served ourselves. When we all had our food, Father began talking.

"I know you have a lot of questions that you'd like to ask me. But it will be awhile before I know all the answers myself. But I do know that I was wrong for deserting you the way I did. And I do know that it was weak of me to run away. God gave me a big responsibility as a husband and father. And when I thought I had a right to give up, I should have sought God's help instead. Had I trusted him as I should have, things would have been different.

"But, thanks to God, you have become more than you were when I left. I can tell that all of you are stronger and more mature. On the other hand, I returned to you less than I was before I left. The farther I went from home, the farther I drifted from God. As a result, I became weaker and weaker, but in the light of God's grace and forgiveness, I'm growing again.

"You may also be wondering how I could desert you if I loved you. Well, when I first heard the story of Peter's denial of Jesus Christ, the same question came to my mind. Peter loved Jesus. He even declared to Jesus that he would lay down his life for Him. But Peter didn't know himself the way he thought he did, because later, during a time of fear, he denied Jesus three times all in one night. But the resurrected Savior gave him three opportunities to declare his love and recommit to his calling, as He restored him to the ministry.

"Christ has forgiven me, and I'm asking you to do the same. I still have some growing to do. But now I know that I can't make things perfect but must put my trust in God, instead of myself, to strengthen and guide me and all of us. And I know that there are some things that only He can change."

"Was that you who passed in front of the house last winter on the day that we got all that snow?" I asked, not knowing where I got the courage.

"Yes, Hon," he answered.

"You saw him and didn't tell us?" Sammy reprimanded.

"That's okay," Mother mediated. "Let him continue."

"When I reached the driveway leading to the side porch, I couldn't come any closer. I didn't feel worthy of coming in and warming myself by the fire made with wood I didn't help cut.

Then, looking at Mother, he added, "Especially since you returned all the checks I mailed you, Clara. It didn't seem fair that I was spending the summer in abundance and plenty while you endured dying crops and an empty harvest."

"We were all right," Mother responded, appearing to be a bit more assured. Then, eager to share some good news with us, she prompted him. "Tell us what you told me. Well, you know, tell them all of it!"

"Well," he started, "I had no plans when I left. I just kept going until I ended up in the place where I found and married your mother. The crops yielded abundantly that summer, so I always found plenty of work there.

"At harvest time, there was this church festival that I attended with the family for whom I was working. There were wagonloads of men, women, and children gathered in a clearing in the center of a grove of trees. It was a beautiful and joyful place. The ground was painted with a carpet of blazing red and gold leaves, while some still clung to the branches of the trees. The autumn breeze was crisp, and small, energetic children chased each other back and forth, laughing and shouting in high-pitched, excited voices.

"The men and older boys placed boards over sawhorses to make tables. Then the women and girls covered them with white sheets and emptied boxes upon boxes of carefully and beautifully prepared food. Chickens had been hand-plucked, cut into pieces, and fried to a crisp, golden brown. Sweet potatoes had been dug and transformed into golden-crusted pies. Blackberries picked and canned earlier in the season were now delicious cobblers.

"When everyone came together to form a circle around the tables to give thanks, a woman stood across from me who looked so much like your mother that it scared me. For a split second I wondered if by some unexplained event she was there. She was smiling, and I could see that she even had dimples like your mother. But she laughed and talked with the people as if they lived among each other and had shared many everyday experiences.

"Even more puzzling was the fact that she was dressed differently from anyone else. And on top of that, the dress she wore was just like the one your mother likes to wear on special Sundays, only hers had different colors in the apron and the ruffle over her shoulders.

"It took courage, but I went up and introduced myself and told her that she looked just like my wife.

"'What's your wife's name?' she asked.

"'Clara,' I said.

"Then she studied my face as if to search for some proof that what seemed to be happening was real. Tears flowed from her eyes. She excused herself and left. I later learned that she was Mrs. Harris, the pastor's wife.

The next day she came to see me at the place where I worked and told me who she was and that her first name was Minnie. She told me that she was your mother's sister and how the two of you had been separated all these years. I'll let her tell you what kept her from finding you, Clara. It's a long story.

Then, with a broad grin on his face, he eagerly reached into his shirt pocket where there had been a soft bulge. He almost shouted, "I forgot something, Clara. I gave you the letter, but there's something else."

Waving a packet wrapped in brown paper and tied with a blue ribbon, he continued. "She told me to give you these. They're zinnia seeds from you mother's garden!"

Chapter Fifteen

The Confession

THAT SUNDAY WE all rode to church together; Father and Mother were up front, and Sammy, Florence, and I were in the back seat. After church, Father went over to visit Uncle Willis, and Sammy went with him to play ball with Jimmy and their friends. Florence spent the afternoon on the front porch swing with Larry, Reverend Freeman's son.

Mother called me to come and read with her. Although the spring air was not steamy as it would be later in the season, and the sun had almost set, we still went to the shady side of the house.

We read the verses about Peter that Father told us about at the table the day before. Then she told me how she had written a letter to Aunt Minnie so that they could plan when they were going to meet.

"I think we'll probably meet back home where we grew up. She says Mother and Father want to see me," my mother said with happy eyes squinting and her dimples deepening as she smiled.

At that moment, with things going so well and seeing all the blessings that God was bestowing on Mother and all of us, I found the courage to tell her about my prayer.

"Mother," I began.

"Yes, Hon?"

"Do you remember that Saturday last summer when Reverend and Mrs. Freeman came to visit you?" I asked.

"Yes, I do," she spoke, searching my face for more information.

"Well, the night before they came, I prayed for God to send you a special patch of rain over your zinnia garden, because I was afraid of what might happen to you if all the flowers died. But God didn't answer my prayer."

"But, He *did* answer your prayer, Hon," she insisted. "You see, when Reverend and Mrs. Freeman came, they brought the Bible and read scripture after scripture about the Living Water that Reverend Freeman spoke about in his sermon that next day. And he read to me a very special passage that was just the promise from God that I needed to hear.

"Open your Bible," she commanded excitedly as she hurriedly turned the pages of hers. "Turn to Isaiah 58:11 and read."

My fingers fumbled through the pages until I finally came to the passage. It read:

The Lord will guide you continually,
And satisfy your soul in drought,
And strengthen your bones;

As I read, I could see what Mother meant. But as I came to the next part, I could see even more clearly why this was a spiritual answer to my earthly prayer. It read:

You shall be like a watered garden,
And like a spring of water, whose waters
do not fail.

We both smiled, and at the same time said, "Amen."

Father never left again. Instead, he and Mother grew closer. And with Reverend Freeman's counsel and with all of us praying, studying, and worshipping together, we got through all our hardships with the strength we received from God.

A special thing happened that summer. There was a period of time when the rains became sparse, as they had the summer before, and the earth became dry and cracked as before. One day, as I sat on the porch steps watching the sky for a hint of a cloud, Father came and sat beside me. I think he must have known that I needed the reassurance of his presence. I was enjoying resting secure against his shoulder when he nudged me and pointed to the western horizon.

"There's a little cloud," he chuckled. "It looks like it is no bigger than my hand. But that doesn't mean it can't bring rain." Sure enough, it grew closer and closer and larger and larger. By the time it reached our house and the fields around us, it began to shower us with soft raindrops.

Father arose in a hurry, went inside, and came back, tugging Mother behind him. They pranced together to the center of the garden, laughing and holding hands. They tilted their faces heavenward as the water formed sheets of glaze over their skin, flowing into the corners of their eyes and down their cheeks. They lifted their hands up in praise, letting the water splash over their palms.

A rumble of thunder sent them rushing back to the porch and into the house. Mother grabbed my hand and tugged me along. Sammy soon rushed in with his drenched shirt clinging to his narrow shoulders flashing a broad smile at Father. Before long a flash of lightning sent Florence and Reverend Freeman's son rushing in from the front porch swing. Inside the shelter of their room, we watched the cloud grow darker, obscuring the bright sun. Flashes of lightning danced across the sky, and the oak tree swayed in the wind. The boards of the barn creaked, and the rain grew faster with the thundering sound of stampeding hooves on the tin roof. Water dripped from the leaves of the zinnias, their newly drenched stems and unopened blossoms standing straight as they were filled with new life. Water flowed into the cracks of the parched earth, overflowing abundantly into streams rushing on to the surrounding earth.

Our lives that summer and summers to come overflowed with both spiritual and earthly plenty.

"So, sweetheart, what can you and I do this very moment?"

Without hesitation and with the dimples deepening into her cheeks, she said, "Pray."

Scripture References
for Further Reading

Chapter 3

'The Lord is my shepherd"—Psalm 23:1
"In the beginning God created"—Genesis 1:1
"Rise Peter"—Acts 10:13
"Jesus wept"—John 11:35
"The story of the lost son"—Luke 15:11-32

Chapter 8

The account of Elijah—1 Kings 17:1-18:46; James 5:17
"Let there be"—Genesis: 1:1-31

Chapter 9

God stated that everything was good—Genesis 1:1-31
Christ will return—John 14:1-3; 1 Thessalonians 4:16-17
Creation groans—Romans 8:18-22
Creation waits—Romans 8-19

Chapter 10

The righteous prosper—Psalms 37:25; Proverbs 13:25

Chapter 11

The story of Samson—Judges 13:1-16:31
The story of Ruth—Ruth 1:1-4:22

Additional Eternal Benefits of Suffering

Psalms 34:18
Hebrews 12:1-11
Romans 8:16-17
2 Corinthians 1:8-10
2 Corinthians 4:17-18
James 1:2-4
1 Peter 5:10-11

CPSIA information can be obtained at www.ICGtesting.com
Printed in the USA
LVOW131930051112

305962LV00001B/3/P